Notes for adults

TADPOLES NURSERY RHYMES are structured to provide support for newly independent readers. The books may also be used by adults for sharing with young children.

The language of nursery rhymes is often already familiar to an emergent reader, so the opportunity to see these rhymes in print gives a highly supportive early reading experience. The alternative rhymes extend this reading experience further, and encourage children to play with language and try out their own rhymes.

If you are reading this book with a child, here are a few suggestions:

1. Make reading fun! Choose a time to read when you and the child are relaxed and have time to share the story.
2. Recite the nursery rhyme together before you start reading. What might the alternative rhyme be about? Why might the child like it?
3. Encourage the child to reread the rhyme, and to retell it in their own words, using the illustrations to remind them what has happened.
4. Point out together the rhyming words when the whole rhymes are repeated on pages 12 and 22 (developing phonological awareness will help with decoding language) and encourage the child to make up their own alternative rhymes.
5. Give praise! Remember that small mistakes need not always be corrected.

First published in 2008 by
Franklin Watts
338 Euston Road
London NW1 3BH

Franklin Watts Australia
Level 17/207 Kent Street
Sydney NSW 2000

Text (Wee Willie Winkie on Mars)
© Wes Magee 2008
Illustration © Martin Remphry 2008

The rights of Wes Magee to be identified as the author of Wee Willie Winkie on Mars and Martin Remphry as the illustrator of this Work have been asserted in accordance with the Copyright, Designs and Patents Act, 1988.

ISBN 978 0 7496 8024 4 (hbk)
ISBN 978 0 7496 8030 5 (pbk)

Series Editor: Jackie Hamley
Series Advisor: Dr Hilary Minns
Series Designer: Peter Scoulding

Printed in China

Franklin Watts is a division of Hachette Children's Books an Hachette Livre UK company.
www.hachettelivre.co.uk

Wee Willie Winkie

Retold by Wes Magee
Illustrated by Martin Remphry

FRANKLIN WATTS
LONDON•SYDNEY

Martin Remphry

"My son Leon loves bedtime stories, especially if they are about fire engines or spaceships. But I always make sure I finish reading them before eight o'clock."

Wee Willie Winkie
runs through the town,

Upstairs and downstairs

in his night-gown.

Rapping at the window,

crying through the
lock,

"Are the children
all in bed ...

... for now

it's eight o'clock?"

Wee Willie Winkie

Wee Willie Winkie
runs through the town,
Upstairs and downstairs
in his night-gown.
Rapping at the window,
crying through the lock,
"Are the children all in bed
for now it's eight o'clock?"

Can you point to the
rhyming words?

Wee Willie Winkie on Mars

by Wes Magee
Illustrated by Martin Remphry

Wes Magee

"Perhaps one day you'll be able to fly on a spaceship to the Moon ... or even to planet Mars!"

Wee Willie Winkie
flies to the stars,

Sends the children off
to bed on planet Mars.

17

Flying to the planet
puts his head into a spin.

So he flies back
to bed ...

... and his mum tucks him in.

Wee Willie Winkie

Wee Willie Winkie
flies to the stars,
Sends the children off
to bed on planet Mars.

Flying to the planet
puts his head into a spin.
So he flies back to bed
and his mum tucks him in.

Can you point to the
rhyming words?

Puzzle Time!

Can you tell the time on these clocks?

Answers

Four o'clock

Half past one

Seven o'clock

Three o'clock

Half past eight

Half past nine